This book is given with love

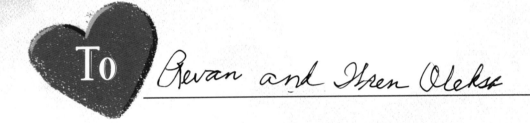

To _Revan and Ihren Oleksa_

From

Grand Mary and Grand Dave

SHERRY THE HARE
DOESN'T
KNOW
HOW TO
SHARE

Written by:
Dr. Barbara Howard &
Anne Marie Brown

Illustrated by:
Carlos Varejão

FOREWARD

This charming book features Sherry the Hare who, like many young children, enjoys and collects special things. But Sherry has not yet figured out the greater social value of sharing with others. Rather than pound home this lesson from a parent, teacher, sibling or peer, Sherry's possessions are washed away by water from a storm. She finds compassion from the same forest creatures she snubbed, and they share the things she needs without question or preaching.

As a Developmental-Behavioral Pediatrician I see families feeling they have to lecture their children to get them to develop moral understandings that are better facilitated by experiences. Even an "I told you so" can backfire with children who may reject the lesson rather than concede their power by admitting they were wrong in how they were acting. This simple story gets the point across with engaging characters and the gift of silent acceptance.

- Dr. Howard

ABOUT DR. HOWARD

Dr. Barbara Howard is a Developmental-Behavioral Pediatrician and an Assistant Professor of Pediatrics at The Johns Hopkins University School of Medicine. She earned her M.D. at Johns Hopkins and trained with Aldrich Award Winner Dr. T. Berry Brazelton at Harvard University. Howard herself won the American Academy of Pediatrics' (AAP's) C. Anderson Aldrich Award in October of 2019, for outstanding contributions to developmental and behavioral pediatrics.

Sherry the Hare,
A wild mountain hare,
Is a lot like a bunny,
But bigger, I swear.

She hops through the forest
With hoppity flair.
But Sherry's one problem,
Is she simply won't share.

She collects all her treasures
Like small, shiny rocks.
Her burrow is brimming
With wondrous stock.

The feathers! The sea shells!
A bottle cap, too.
A hairpin, and oak leaves
Of interesting hues.

Three pennies, five chestnuts,
You'll find it all there.
But ask her to see them?
She simply won't share!

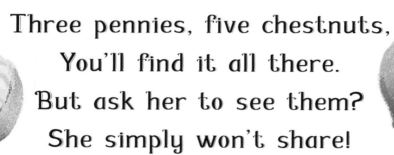

The requests of the forest
Have all been declined.
Give Squirrel a spare acorn?
She wasn't inclined.

When Blue Jay asked Sherry
For fluff for her nest,
Sherry said it was hers
And refused the request.

The Beaver asked Sherry
For sticks for his dam.
Raccoon needed berries,
She told them to...

Sherry the Hare
Does not seem to care
That nobody plays with
This hoppity hare.

But...
One fateful evening,
WHOOSH! Pours the rain!
Her burrow is flooded,
And all she's obtained...

...Is washed down a river
Right out of the wood.
Now Sherry has nothing,
And nothing's no good.

She's in quite a pickle.
No home, and no bed.
No food she can nibble.
A cold night ahead.

She hops to an oak tree,
Asks Squirrel for some nuts.
And Beaver brings timber
To build her a hut.

Blue Jay and Raccoon
Serve Sherry some tea.
She thinks in her hare brain,
"They're helping me?"

Now hoppity Sherry,
A generous hare,
Knows the power of giving,
And the importance of care.

...And if any creature
Needs something, it's theirs!
Now that Sherry the Hare,
Finally learned how to share.

Claim your FREE Gift!

Visit:

PDICBooks.com/Gift

Thank You
for Purchasing

SHERRY THE HARE
DOESN'T KNOW HOW TO SHARE

and welcome to the Puppy Dogs & Ice Cream family.
We're certain you're going to love the little gift
we've prepared for you at the website
listed on the previous page.